Monster Truck Mountain Rescue

Peter Bently

Illustrated by Martha Lightfoot

Mouse is getting ready to **drive**
Monster Truck at a rally.

Mouse puts on his fireproof suit and **safety** helmet,
then checks the **giant** tyres and suspension.

Mouse drives Monster Truck into the stadium
and pulls up ready for the race.
Mouse revs the engine.

VROOM!

VROOM!

The announcer says,
"Ready, get set, GO!"
Bang! The starter pistol fires.
Monster Truck is off!

Monster Truck **races** down the track.

ROAR!

CRUNCH!

It **bounces** easily over a pile of cars.

BOING!

"Yippee, way to go!" cries Mouse.

CRASH!

Mouse and Monster Truck **crush** an old bus
as *flat* as a pancake.

SMASH!

They **charge** through a line of caravans.

HURRAY!

Finally Mouse does a wheelie and **flies** over the finish line.

Monster Truck is the winner!

Mouse and Monster Truck
drive **home** with their prize.

A police car
and fire engine
are **blocking** the road.

An avalanche has **destroyed** the bridge
and there's a climber stuck up the mountain.

The rescue helicopter **arrives**...

...but it can't land because of the wind.
"How will we **save** the climber now?"
asks the Fire Chief.

Monster Truck **races** up the mountain.
It **climbs** over huge rocks and boulders.

SPLOSH!

Mouse **plunges** across a deep river.
Monster Truck's big wheels keep Mouse safe and dry.

Monster Truck **reaches** the climber.
Mouse carefully **helps** her down.

The weather gets **worse.**
They can't go back the way they came.

Monster Truck charges back down the mountain.
They reach the **broken** bridge.

Mouse **knows** what he has to do...

He backs up, **revs** the engine, then puts his foot down on the accelerator.

The engine **growls**, the wheels spin, and Monster Truck shoots forward.

"Thank you for **RESCUING** me!" says the climber.

Everyone **congratulates** Mouse.

"And well done Monster Truck!"
grins Mouse.

Let's look at
Monster Truck

Driver's cage

Flag

Exhaust pipe

Giant tyres

Driver's
seat

Safety
harness

Engine

Suspension

Frame

Other Monster Vehicles

Monster car

Monster motorbike

Monster bus

For my lovely brothers, Tobin & Luke. M.L.
For Eli. P.B.

Designer: Plum5 Limited
Project Editor: Lucy Cuthew
Editorial Assistant: Tasha Percy

First published in the UK in 2013 by
QED Publishing
A Quarto Group company
230 City Road
London EC1V 2TT

www.qed-publishing.co.uk

A catalogue record for this book is available from the British Library.

ISBN: 978 1 78171 092 0

Printed in China